QUIVERING LAND

QUIVERING LAND

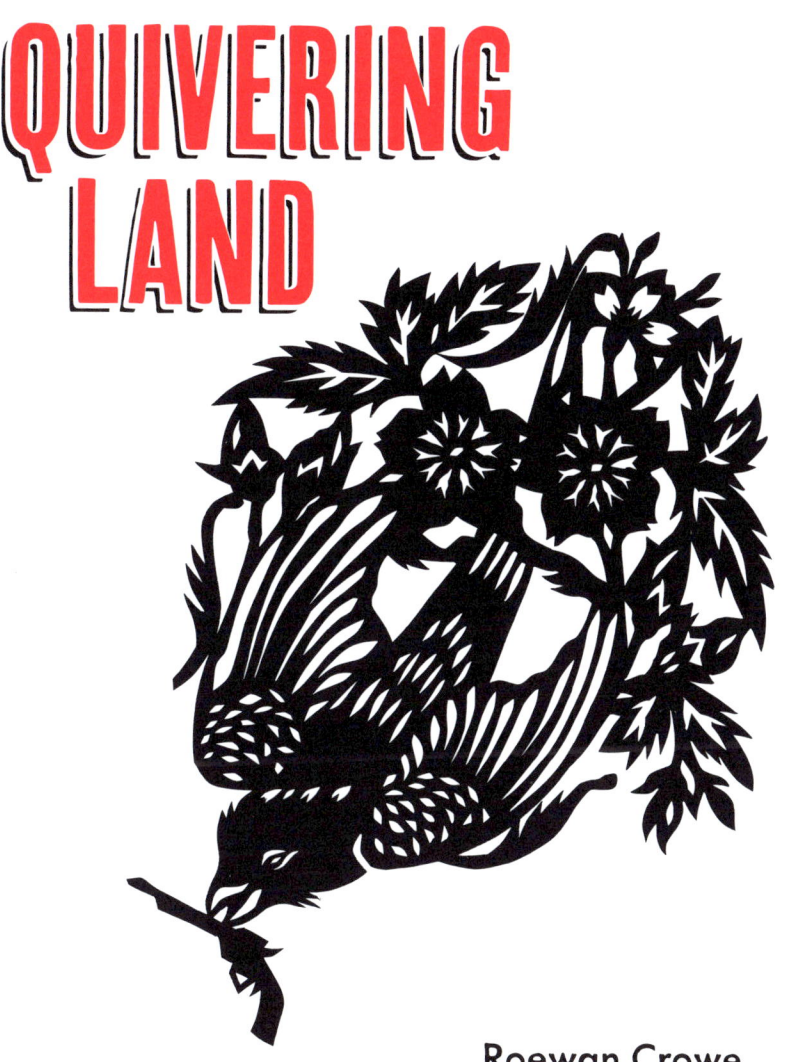

Roewan Crowe

ARP BOOKS • WINNIPEG, MB

Poetry is the liquid voice that can wear through stone.

—*Adrienne Rich*

the eyes' trace at the root of thought
emotive colour
I draw myself close because
what is change toward there
a speakable vulnerability
in this site
I'll talk of the horizon

—*Nicole Brossard*

I don't know why, but those words I just said
brought me to tears.

—*Marguerite Duras*

Copyright ©2013 Roewan Crowe

ARP BOOKS (Arbeiter Ring Publishing)
201E-121 Osborne Street
Winnipeg, Manitoba
Canada R3L 1Y4
arpbooks.org

Printed in Canada by Kromar Printing
Design by Mike Carroll
Cover image by Paul Robles

COPYRIGHT NOTICE
This book is fully protected under the copyright laws of Canada and all other countries of the Copyright Union and is subject to royalty. Any properly footnoted quotation of up to five hundred sequential words may be quoted without permission, so long as the total number of words does not exceed two thousand. For longer continuous quotations or for a greater number of words, contact Arbeiter Ring Publishing for permission.

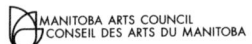

 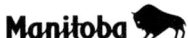

ARP acknowledges the financial support of our publishing activities by Manitoba Culture, Heritage, and Tourism, and the Government of Canada through the Canada Book Fund.

ARP acknowledges the support of the Province of Manitoba through the Book Publishing Tax Credit and the Book Publisher Marketing Assistance Program.

We acknowledge the support of the Canada Council for our publishing program.

With the generous support of the Manitoba Arts Council.

Printed on paper from 100% recycled post-consumer waste.

LIBRARY AND ARCHIVES CANADA CATALOGUING IN PUBLICATION

Crowe, Roewan, author
    Quivering land / Roewan Crowe ; Paul Robles, illustrator.

ISBN 978-1-894037-90-7 (pbk.)

I. Robles, Paul, 1969-, illustrator II. Title.

PS8605.R6935Q83 2013   C818'.6   C2013-905622-X

CONTENTS

12	Her Western Landscape
22	Drifting along Tumbling Tumbleweed
28	Unforgiven
39	Each and Every Bullet
41	Dead Men (The Exhibit)
46	Monument Valley
52	Shadow Play
56	Ghost Action
64	Everything
65	Wooden Word
70	High Noon
83	Bullet Toss
88	Emptied Chamber
89	Stone Child
92	Lucky Lady Saloon
101	Her Shadow Dancing
102	Stone Horse
106	Herd of Wild
114	Inside
118	The Question of Being Fenced In
122	Thundering Hooves
127	Night Sky
129	Lifting Stone
133	Pressed Flowers
136	Shifting Ground
140	Site Specific
144	Don't Take Your Guns to Town
154	Horizon
173	The Sun Setting
177	With Gratitude
181	Biographies

IMAGES
by Paul Robles

10	*Dislocation*
27	*Evidence*
45	*Mother (Abattoir Totem #1)*
54	*Ambushed*
69	*Lost Hope*
86	*Reclamation*
91	*Ghost Offering*
105	*Haunted*
112	*Father (Abattoir Totem #2)*
121	*Menace*
135	*Wallflowers*
142	*Aftermath*
153	*Abandoned/Hope (Version #1)*

for my sweet, fierce love
Jarvis

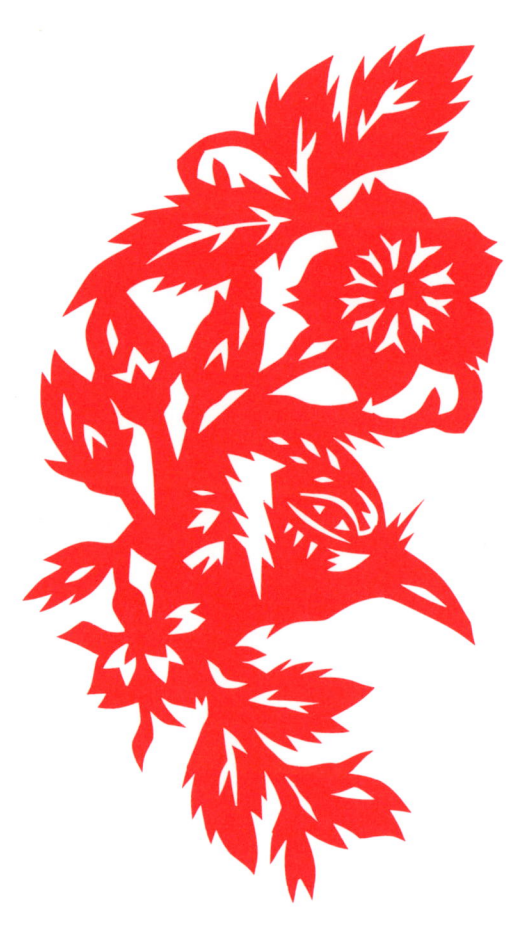

i walk the line. the horizon line.

HER WESTERN LANDSCAPE

Clem alone in the house her father built
      edge of town

a simple structure
door, four windows
table and chairs
large bed in the corner

each thing in proper order

Clem's boots, thinking hard
bare wooden floor
back and forth, each step a consideration

her determined turn
to outside
shoulder to door
pushing open

wind against her
unsettling

Out front an old tree
its trunk curved by the wind

Leg high and over
she's swinging

back of horse
speckled hide, hooves
ground beneath

shifting clouds, birds

      restless
riding landscape

        horizon
              line, quivering with the sun

Clem, horse
their bodies carving
red sandstone buttes

                history

    rock   formations

searching

She sleeps under the dark sky
not the soft bed in the empty house

leg high and over dawn
riding, again
pushing into the wind
leaving the valley

circling, circling
the western town

She can't enter the town
steady four-beat pace
'round mean outskirts
near hind, near fore, off hind, off fore
until it's time to rest her horse

Faithfully, she returns
to father's abandoned house

missing family
      on the edge of this

           necessary repetition

Out back of the house, gravesite

don't move, she mouths
stand tight, dead still
as if she was dead
buried here

instead of this delicate skeleton

      dead bird
           stiff beak shut wings splayed

          like it had
              fallen

Clem shades eyes from wide and blue

        she dug a small hole in the dirt. gathered blades of quackgrass dandelion greens. placed daisies under clawed feet. johnny jump-ups under wings. fashioned a grassy pillow for its little head. humming a song for its dead beauty.

one palmful of dirt, then another
until   feathered body covered

Mother's voice interrupting
yank of Clem's arm

      Leave what's dead alone

DRIFTING ALONG TUMBLING TUMBLEWEED

Violet reaches to turn off the teevee, but she doesn't. Instead she turns down the volume, watching the stage coach hustle and bump through Monument Valley, chased by men on horses with arrows flying, guns firing back at them, dust and death everywhere.

She hauls her body off the couch, back to the workbench at the centre of her studio. Stands there. Contemplating the dead, recalling each gun and bullet, each body falling heavy to the ground. She's been seized tight by this story, held captive by the heroic western tale, old stories about Cowboys and Indians, dusty towns, loaded guns, and the jagged pink landscape of Monument Valley.

She wanders over to the small fridge and pours a glass of cool clear water into her silver cup. Johnny Guitar sings the ballad of Little Jo while riding through the desert on a buckboard. A Dead Man, searching and pale, rides the High Plains Drifting.

Now she's drifting, drifting like a tumbleweed blown across the land, scattering seeds in her room.

She thinks about the rugged hero, dangerous and lonely with thickened scars and a hidden past that keeps busting through the narrative. A lone maverick who saves the town and rides away, free from love and its trappings, rides into the landscape, just him and his horse.

    And lonely, always lonely.

> Did I say I was lonely?

Violet drinks from the cup, closing her eyes. How did these Hollywood men settle in her psyche, capture her imagination? John Wayne, Clint Eastwood, Henry Fonda, Gary Cooper, Paul Newman and Robert Redford. Celluloid heroes, packing iron at their side, all with tall boots and few words to speak.

When they do, they keep saying the same things over and over. She finds this soothing, their failure to utter something new deeply reassuring.

Actions speak louder than words.

Returning to the teevee, Violet finds John Wayne, towering on the screen. He's the tallest man by far, as tall as the rock formations in the desert of Tsé Bii Ndzisgaii, Valley of the Rocks, Sand Dunes Around the Rock Formations—Monument Valley. Why has she attached herself so fiercely to this land of the Navajo? What did this place come to mean for John Wayne? John Ford?

Now the Duke leans into the doorframe of a settler's house, leans into her studio.

What is this threshold between a wooden house and an open sky? Outside, the wilderness, the frontier, is where it is said that a new life might begin again. Violet returns her gaze; she has watched this scene with John Wayne over and over and tries to remember the ending before it happens again.

> Does he walk away? For good?

Her memory sense tells her this is a substantial gesture. Before she can fully recall, she watches him turn, walk away into the wind—door left wide open, the outside spilling in. How the doorframe shapes everything, enclosing meaning as if meaning might be contained within straight lines. What does it mean to deviate from the line drawn out for you, the line you are supposed to follow? What does it mean to follow the line?

Is the horizon a straight line?

The lines, these rigid frames have held the broken treaties, massacres, land by fraud, land by force, women by force, the army, missionaries, relocations, hangings of the warriors who fought back.

Lines drawn on the land.

The happened is still happening.
She wants to slam it.

> *ride away, ride away, ride away*

Standing at the threshold, she watches him ride away.
Looks into the space he left.

The land was not empty.
The soil not virgin.

Is there a home, or a sunset to ride into?

There is a sun. It still sets.

haunting subject

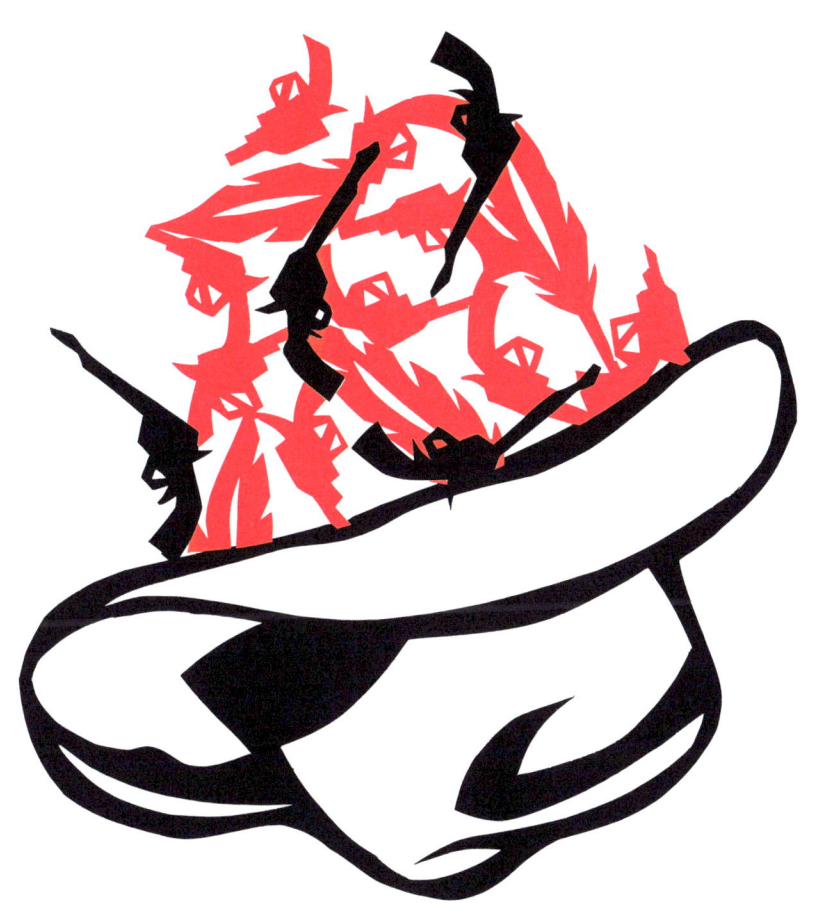

UNFORGIVEN

The mud, the rain
Clem, her mare

story tucked under

        interrupting. or is it a blast? history demands its place in the narrative. what do we want from the past?

clenched horn of saddle

it might have been
        loud crack of thunder

caused Clem
to finally ride the past
cross the line drawn in red dry dirt

maybe it was the rain-drenched stranger
Clem watched ride into town
        dismount from his horse

as if only now she could imagine doing the same

Clem rides clip clop over
wooden bridge, thirsty creek
right down main street
past the place where the hardware store used to be
past the bank built of brick

toward cowboy, only other rider on the street

Clem feels odd
out of time
        deserted place

tightens reins to stop
feet land on hardened dirt, hitching horse

there, there out front of saloon
lifeless bodies propped up
rough wooden coffins

heinous display

        stranger standing beside her

Clem feels mouth   opening

    Those are my folks

feel feet, earth, beneath boots
search for response: none
stranger's face lowered

    Those are my folks

man looks up at Clem
cold, blank stare
steady stream of rain falling
falling from the brim of his hat
    every cowboy starts to cry

how many sinister towns has he ridden through?
how many times has he turned his head to the past?
raised his rifle in revenge?

bang
bang
lower your head to the dead

Unbuckling his saddlebag
sound of her undoing

pulling out leather holster and pistol
tossing it to Clem

she straps it on
buckles rig snug

        hips buzz

Everything loaded

Walking past dead mother, dead father
smell sickening

mother's body slumping face sunken pale

father's face gentle
even with life blown out of him

Clem wants to stop, reach over
touch them

        whatever would she say?

She follows the cowboy into the saloon
legs shaking, each step uncertain

yet confidence grows with   looming shadow
ten-gauge double-barreled rifle

Clem tallies the faces of the men
the mayor
the bosses
the hustlers
the cowards

the Law

she tentatively pulls out
Colt, 1860 Army

setting her aim on the one wearing the gold star

eye for an eye

There, there
he is raising hands in fake surrender
Clem's eyes meet his mocking
could she kill him?

    Are you gonna pull that trigger, or just think about it?

she   cocks   back

hammer

It is the strange Man
No Name
who shoots

      dry click of rifle

Clem's heart tightens, falters

misfire, no bullets exit from chambers

she steadies her aim
—could kill him—

this possibility radiates from gun
      in shaking grip

she feels dangerous
      everything glows

She doesn't fire
Man with No Name
draws Scofield

Boom
Boom
Boom
Boom
Boom

men's bodies
fall fast
heavy
        to wooden floor

One
Two
Three
Four
Five men

dead
—just like that—

Roar of gun smashes through her body
hole in Law's chest where his heart used to be

she stumbles outside
past rotting family

tries to shake
shake
the sound, the smell, death

count
1-2-3-4-5 6-7

can't feel edges of her self
see past borders
of this violent

                                                                                     (family)

EACH AND EVERY BULLET

Standing on the edge of the horizon
a young girl takes each and every bullet into her heart
catching the odd stray with her tiny teeth.

Not as dark as ripened cherry
Darker than crisp red apple
Richer than throat of red gladiolus
More vibrant than blazing sunset
The colour of fresh blood

>> Her dress dirty: yes
>> Her dress bloodied: yes

If you asked the girl she would say her red dress wasn't always this way.

In front of her is the town, ablaze with gunfire
behind her

>>> —Monument Valley

giant stones standing with sky.

(these curved lines, this stone embrace, holding her insides)

DEAD MEN (THE EXHIBIT)

Violet blasts the white walls with bullet holes. Rubs the lip of each hole with charcoal and oil pastel, heightening their depth.

She drags the dead men into the gallery. Bloody tracks on wooden floors, she's standing knee deep in the guts of the Hollywood Western, guts of the West. Dead weight, heavy weight, she props each one of the bodies against a wall.

> Blood oozing.
> This repetition.

Near the door, on the farthest wall she applies words in black vinyl,

> "I don't know who is right and who's wrong,
> there's got to be some better way to live."

She steels her nerves, calls in the ghosts, everyone out from the shadows.

Turns on the sound until gunshots send vibrations throughout the space. Standing there, she counts bullet holes. One of the bodies slides down to the floor. Violet props it up again. Hands on hips she stops, stares. Decides to return the body to where it has slid down.

Then counts.

The gallery assistant comes up behind her, *any trouble?*
> *Thought I was having trouble with my adding, it's alright now.*

During the opening, in the midst of this deathly display, artists, strangers, and friends congratulate her. There is much laughter, small talk, booze, and celebration.

At the end of the evening Violet reads the comments written in the guest book:
> Congratulations!
> Great show!
> Depressing and dark.
> Congrats Violet, good work!
> There should have been popcorn, just like the movies.
> Did you use real blood?
> When will the bodies decompose?
> Isn't the Western dead?
> I don't understand how you can create something so violent.
> Do you hate men?
> Who is the signifier who pulled the trigger?
> Cowboys! Where are the Indians?
> Make sure you stop by my show next week.
> Do you think there is a western revival going on?
> Why did you only display the bodies of men?
> Why did you only use white men?
> Hah! Those men aren't only white.

i've watched every hollywood western movie clint eastwood has ever starred in or directed. we met the other night at a greasy spoon diner. it was late. we were both eating huge pieces of lemon meringue pie. filling was lemony tart, fluffy meringue so high it almost toppled over. i said to him, "i think we are wrestling with some of the same issues in our work." when he looked at me, it was as if he wasn't really there, his eyes emptied with each bullet he had fired.

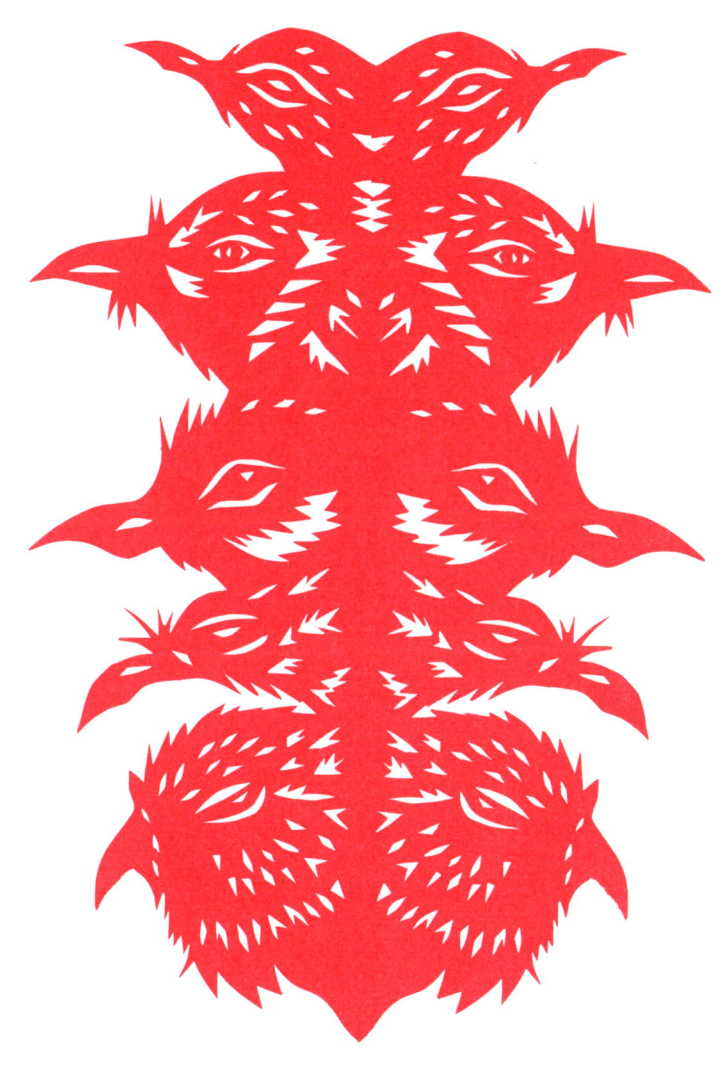

MONUMENT VALLEY

Narrowing passages, towering buttes
sun setting as it always does

twisting hair around her fingers
every now and again sucking on the ends
trembling with terror of the unforgiven

she reaches into darkness
traces edges

stone curves
sculpted by sand, wind
sun and rain

her fingers   ancient
touch   stone

each layer holding a story

—a story—

Layers of shale on the inside
        her mom, her dad

                (there were no goodbyes)

—a small bird—
        sandstone wings

ridged stories shudder beneath touch
fins and arches rise from the sandy valley

Law
stands
hard
inside her

then No Name
staring her down
mean squint
red bruised scars riding high on his cheeks

I got scars too
she whispers into stone spires

She doesn't linger
heads deep into the valley
retreats to the Colt
Man with No Name bravado

his lethal ways impress Clem
she might even use the word—worship

though if pressed she would surely crow
she doesn't worship anybody

each
in the end
just a pile of blood and bones

Path widening through twisted trees
sandstone mesas
      silence
      witness

                          sky

Clem looks up
blue deepening

gentle back and forth of horse

Up ahead
shadowy shape beneath arch of stone
single horse and rider

Clem rides toward the shadow
       it does not move

she rides through it
       no one, nothing

on the ground
crescent hoof prints filling with sand

       she follows

narrow path, steep incline into ravine
bush mint
black greasewood
purple sage scenting the air

white-stemmed evening primrose
bending with dew

The mare edges down
stones slide
 roll

bone dry riverbed
memory of cool clear water gripped in its banks

    —memory—

tracks end

SHADOW PLAY

Violet searches through cupboards, drawers, small cardboard boxes, looking for just the right thing. She's drawn to lead, charcoal, oil and chalk, finds pencils, sticks and pastels. Pulls out black, variations of grey: cool grey, ash, battleship, slate. Chooses reds: crimson, vermilion, carmine, scarlet.

There is so much riding her, her body hardened by the jangle of spurs, the bodies dead, blood dried on her cheek, absence of something she doesn't understand.

She wants the killing to stop.

Forced marches to stop,
prison camps,
boarding schools.

She wants sunset and flower to mean something again.
Wants to wear a red dress. The trail of tears to end.
For good.

Pulling out large pieces of paper—Violet sets oil and charcoal to page. Quick and fast, lines hard and thick. She draws wounds, one after another, mining of the sacred hills, damming of water, forced exile, loss of children, disappeared women.

She draws the cowboy's return to the small town, a haunted past.
This her wound too, place of continual return.

Riding the land that never belonged to him. Tight inside his chest the incessant sound of rifle, handgun, six shooter.

>	She draws each blast.

He wasn't always alone. He might have ridden with a brother, or best friend, or a gang of lawless men. Until they were all shot. Dead.

She yearns for beautiful. Is weary of her studio's open space incessantly filling with history, death, gunfights.

—shattering cry of the gun—

This death landscape of loss she calls home, seeps in and out of her as she draws another wound.

>	Her own.

She watches it settling across the page.

Its shadow intrigues her.

She stands up to stretch her legs. Walks around the studio, aimless. Turns toward the white wall. Her shadow falling in front of her, now she's up against the wall.

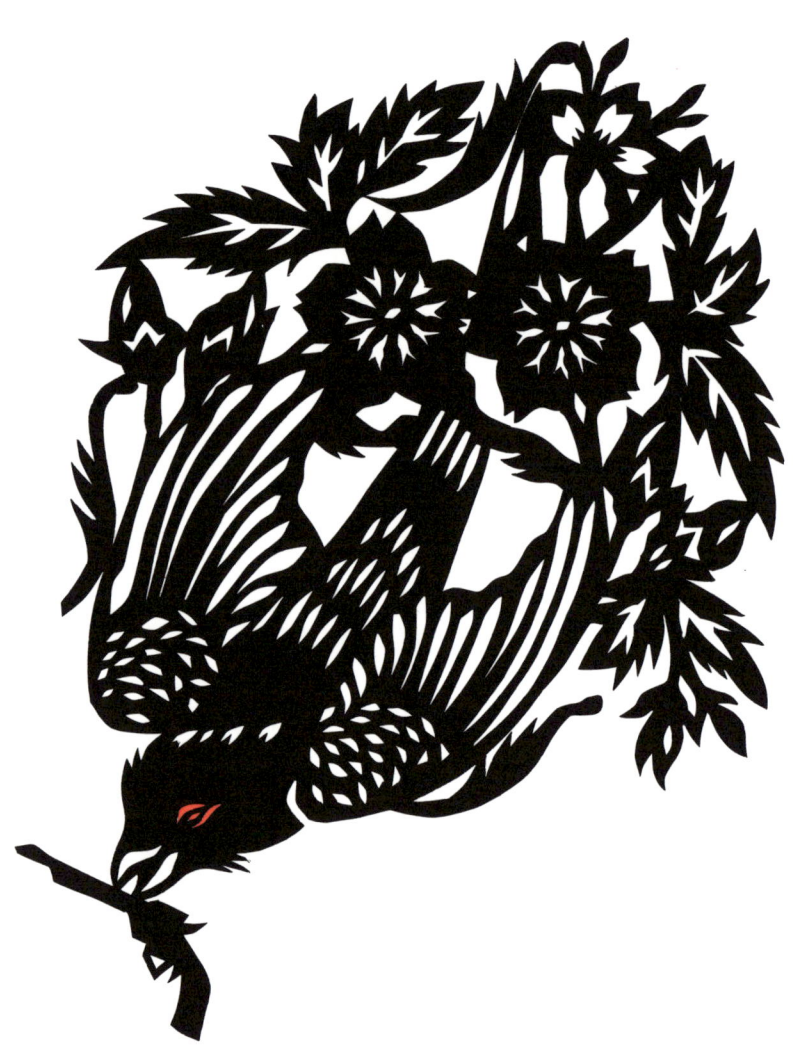

she verb: a Western

GHOST ACTION

With the light of morning Clem returns to the town

unnaturally quiet
just spectral sounds
passing by, passing through

wounds whistling in the wind

she thinks about calling out
        Man with No Name

doesn't want to hear
voice crack plead with wind

laying her hand on the side of the Colt
aching to exit this lonely
mourning with bullet

go ahead
when you have a gun
no one will stop you

Clem draws the Colt, spins around

thing about ghosts
you can shoot 'em full of lead
doesn't make any difference

ricochet
ricochet

down the deserted street
blasting windows
shards of her image falling to the ground

she fires through closed doors, empty buildings
fires a round into the sky

expects someone to yell from a window
come rushing out

but nothing
no one

Heart pounding, she leans against
wooden doorframe
reloads

across the road
flash of silver
figure slumped in corner of doorway

Clem approaches
nudges
jeans faded
feet bare
shirt thin, dirty white cotton
buttons strain
to hold dignity
hips hungry, just bones

ghost?

hand clutched around finest gun belt Clem has ever seen
worn hand-tooled holster
bullets tucked in loops of leather

Clem steps over arm
flung across wooden sidewalk
over leather belt

stands for a moment

walks away   step quickening
afraid she'd be pulled down

at a safe distance, Clem considers her direction
clouds race across the sky
whiteness shadows ground

—deep hush—

paced jangle of spurs

Clem turns back

body remains perfectly still
eyes shut as if kissing for the very first time

a corner of mouth higher on one side
has mouth moved?
did she hear?
dark and damp a piece of hair
Clem leans in to brush it away
is there breath?
do ghosts breathe?

bending ear down to chest
slightest rise and fall

—breath—

as if driven by biting west wind
Clem stands, steps back
      —spits—

—black cowboy boot—

she sees it there poised,
ready to kick
kick

I am in trouble

places foot back on ground

can't make sense of her hatred
for this stranger lying here alone

wrapping one hand around Colt butt
Clem reaches to take the leather belt of bullets

quiet thrust of a hand around Clem's boot

eyes open

Seen enough?
Gonna walk away not knowin' whether I'm dead or alive?
Steal my bullets?
Shoot me?

Clem struggles to free her foot from   peculiar grip
stranger climbs up from the ground, pulling on Clem
registering gun, bloodied shirt

I wouldn't have taken you for a murdering thief
I'm not

notices Clem's cowboy boots, jet black
I'm not.

What size are your feet?

You want my boots? Clem stutters
Ya, I want your boots

You want these bullets, my belt?

And I'm left without boots?

You got feet don't you?

Ya I got feet

Clem pulls off her boots

Well lookie there, you do have feet
stranger slides on Clem's boots, whistles

These boots sure look good on me

stands up tall, dusting off dirt
hands belt to Clem
Hope you ain't the type to hold a grudge

I might be

Clem walks away
tries to hold her stride proud
sharp stones poking at the bottom of her feet
leather belt of bullets swinging beside her

Bye, the stranger sings out
strutting and whistling a haunting tune

Clem takes one last look at the person now in front of the saloon

Hey! the stranger calls out
My friends call me Someone

EVERYTHING

Everything that happened in the western happened to her.

Murdered, left out in the cold, pissed on, spat on, shit on, tortured, scratched, hung, starved, kicked, shot, cut, dragged, whipped, beaten, punched, raped, sold, poisoned, backhanded, ridiculed, humiliated, shamed, stepped on, stomped on, slapped, slashed, burned, left, left for dead.

Everything that happened in the western happened to her.

Sitting at the edge of a polluted stream she tries to get the red dress clean.

THE WOODEN WORD

The word lies wooden in the aftermath of violence.

Hollow and silent.

Violet boots around the wooden word, her father's rifle slung over her shoulder by a worn leather strap. She kicks it, watches the silent word roll in dust and gravel. Too heavy with grief to catch the wind and tumble. She doesn't have the heart to keep laying her boots to it.

She could boot it out of here. Leave this town for good. But she's stuck in this god damn western, caught in its action.

Pulling the rifle snug into her shoulder, she sights the word. Blows it apart.

The rifle repeats.

      Sees her father's face, worn and rugged.

It was so much like John Wayne's, but with more feeling. Her father, a kind man. Closing her eyes, she searches for his image again, inside this blank space where her father used to be.

She watched dusters with him, her small body tucked into the crook of his arm, hands full of popcorn. Teevee screen filling the small space with flickering light and the sound of hooves, creaking leather, showdowns, and gunshots. Good guys, bad guys, or so it seemed.

How tender the times when she read words aloud to him from the teevee guide, hunting magazine, small town paper. Sometimes it was instructions, and together they would assemble a small engine, shed, a lawn mower. Her thirst for words made her young heart oblivious to shame.

Side-by-side they learned. They built walls and fences, installed wood stoves and shingled roofs. Once they wired an old wooden shack with light—it glowed, light spilling out into the darkest night.

Violet can't see her father's face, just the queer blue of her painted fingernails examining the remains of the blasted word, picking up each fragment as if it might help her to better understand the space between them. She doesn't pause to recall her mother, an idea from long ago, instead she notices how sky and water mingle on each fingernail, hold the distance blue, silent.

Like this.

living outside the Law
no protection from the Law
an outlaw is a wild and vicious horse
s/he home free
s/he, a lawless life

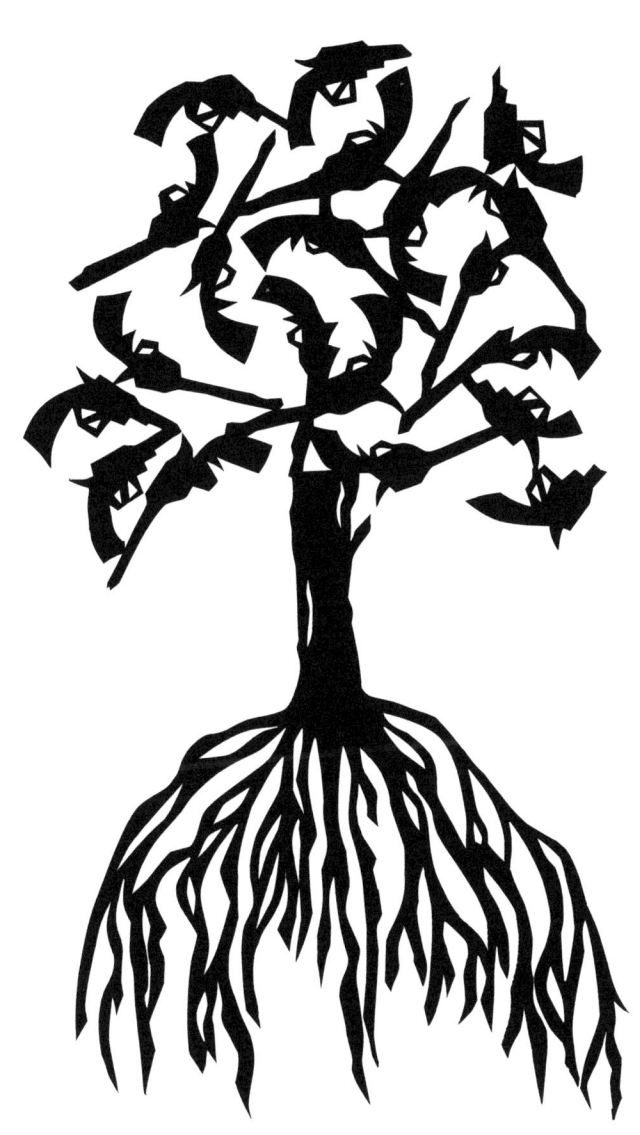

HIGH NOON

Town's main square, oak tree
outstretched limb
knotted rope dropped

Clem joins at the back of crowd
shoulder to shoulder

noose swaying back and forth

in the shadow of the tree
white townsfolk

hangman hooded
fabric hastily hand-sewn
glazed stare from slits

blasted Law standing beside him

Bareback atop a black horse
Someone stripped to waist
hands tied at wrist, resting on horse's neck

oddly calm

Clem figures the noose is dangling at least eight feet

horse will be startled, bolt
rope will tighten
outlaw will

                                        fall

                                      swing

                        from tree   'til dead

Under the noonday sun
Clem, the crowd
everything out in the open
no need to hide vigilante deeds

it's Someone, face grave
who nods to Clem
now pushing through the crowd

trying to get closer

Hooded hangman mounts his horse
places twisted hemp necktie over Someone's head

thirteen coils in a left hand spiral
rope knot digs into ear

Clem swallows hard
checks the clock; almost noon

Final words? hangman asks

I'd like to wear my hat
Get the hat!
crowd shouts, surprising compassion
hangman places hat
black felt, band of silver

Pull the front lower would you?
he adjusts the hat just so

Noon, the Law proclaims

Hangman slapping horse's rear with doubled rope

crowd heaves, gasp
some cheer, some cry out

        horse gallops away

Clem stiff, watching

                              Someone

                s   w   i   n   g   s

crooked Law, his grisly smile

In the din of this grim
sound of girl-child bawling
man dragging her behind him, through the crowd

who brings a kid to a hanging?

Clem snaps, whips
Colt above her head
fires wildly into sky

silence falls
girl stops crying
path opens between

                Clem   the man

                        her voice cuts sharp
                          across vacant dirt

Hey mister, stop hurting her
he glares at Clem

How 'bout you loosen your grip off her arm?
he releases his hold

Clem marshals toward him, gun beginning to glow
You her dad?
he nods yes

Not that it matters
when you're taking care of a child
that's your job
taking care, not doing harm

Clem shoves the barrel of the gun into his chest
hurting him

light from the gun is not blazing
she presses harder
tip digging into his skin

—light fading—

She's just little, see?

Clem doesn't look at the girl, her eyes narrowed
wraps her other hand around the Colt
leaning in, full weight
barrel plunging into the man's sternum

now a reflective surface, a mirror

her image distorted by the barrel's curve
        she sees Clem reflected back
        hard, mean
        her body twisting around the metal

                —small—

his eyes watering, face reddening

Look at how big your hands are
—he does not comply—

Look at your hands!
he looks down at his square hands

Be careful with those damn hands!

Little girl wringing
the edge
of her dress

For emphasis
Clem fires a second shot into the air

Look! a woman yells
Shot went clean through the noose
then pulls the rope from Someone's neck
shouts: She's alive!

Well, stone the crows
Clem tilts her hat back

Someone slides fingers into mouth
sharp whistle—horse returns
and a man heaves Someone
onto back of black horse
then, arm high on horse's neck
reins held loose
galloping away

vigilantes trailing
firing pistol and rifle

Clem and her horse race behind
hand clasping gun, certain
she would have made Man with No Name proud

Someone can't get far! the Law yells
Just a cliff and river on the other side

Horses do not stop
ride into sky

                bits of blue
                freed by hooves

they drop into rushing river

all but Someone,
        now galloping high above them

BULLET TOSS

Girl trotting like horse through sandstone buttes
sliding down sand dunes
skinny coyote at her side
late day sun at their backs.

Dodging yellow mounds of broom snakeweed
patch of desert wolfberry
pops plump red berries into her mouth
dog rolling in the dirt.

Bird darts around them
high above a craggy pillar of ore.

They gallop to moon-like crater, old uranium mine now filled with rain water.

Girl plunges her hands into yellow dust-covered liquid
sucking toxic into her mouth, drinking deeply.

Papery wings of the saltbush offer her seeds to chew on.
She eats the seeds, the salty leaves, drinks more water.

Renewed, girl and coyote tear through the valley
head for the monument of yellow dirt.

They race to the top of the hill
tongues panting
she and coyote digging
toes and claws into sandy stained soil
revealing hundreds of bullets.

Her small hands collect them
from the contaminated heap of dirt
coyote recovers bullets too,
tenderly, with its teeth.

They gather and gather
pile them into a monument
copper, bronze, steel and lead.

Girl and coyote on top of the hill
moon rising above them.

Tossing a bullet up into the air, she shouts

        Heads, I'm dead.
        Tails, I'm not.

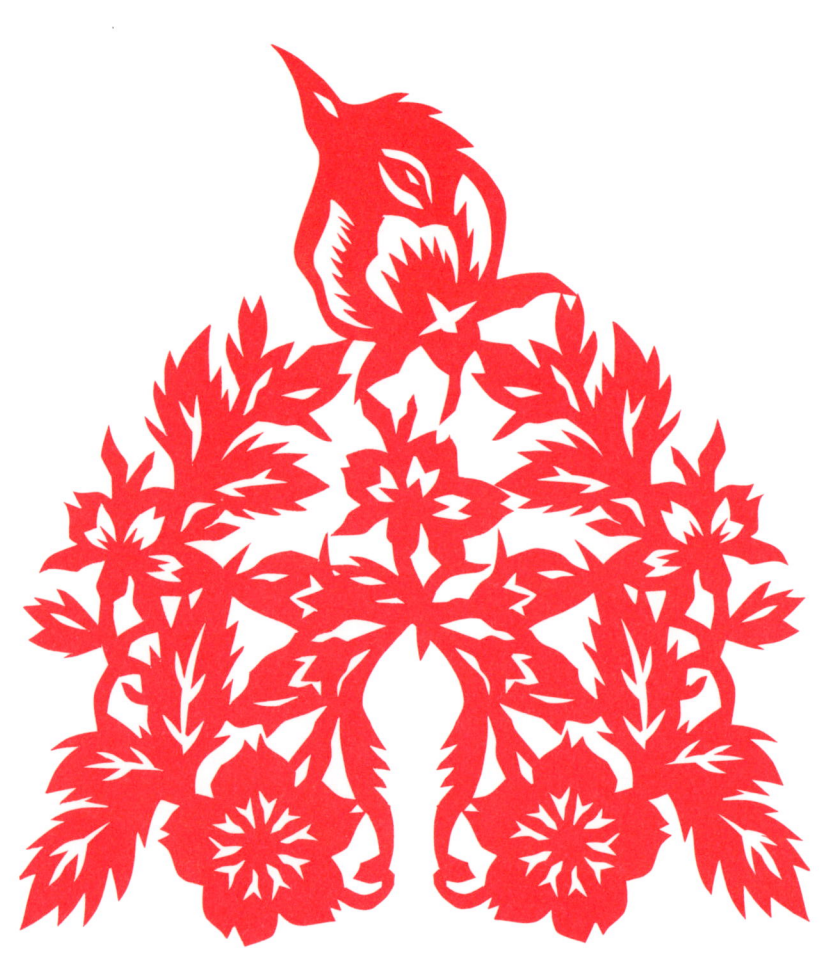

dream: walking into a shower of bullets. arms outstretched. trying to balance a pink peony in my opened palms without the flower being blown apart. pulse at the tender part of my wrists aching, threatening to burst open.

EMPTIED CHAMBER

Clem stands barefoot in the open doorway of the studio.
Leaning into the frame.

Violet is grinding pellets of potassium nitrate.
Crushing charcoal.
Mixing these in her wide mouthed mortar and pestle, she adds sulfur.

Half listening to the grind of black gunpowder, Clem spins the chamber of the revolver.

You know Violet, it's not the dead you have to worry about.

Violet does not respond.

STONE CHILD

She liked to sit on the side of the road, at the edge, where grass meets gravel. Worn overall shorts, faded green, a strap rolling off one shoulder. Her bare legs filthy from playing outside, socks fallen, creased with dirt. Legs pit-marked from stones. Always a scab trying to heal because she wouldn't stop picking at it.

Surrounding her are plastic yellow tobacco containers, vertical ridges running up each side, like ripple potato chips. Inside, gems gathered from the road, sorted by size, shape and colour.

In her hand a hammer. Its wooden handle worn smooth by her dad's hands. With the whack of the hammer and the breath of a silent wish she'd crack open each rock. Inside flakes of silver. Stars in her eyes. Hundreds of glittering rock wishes piling up beside her. Gravel pit of hope.

Each time the same wish. That harm should come to no one, and that she had the power to make it so.

"… rock is as old as the earth is;
stone is only as old as humanity."
— Don McKay

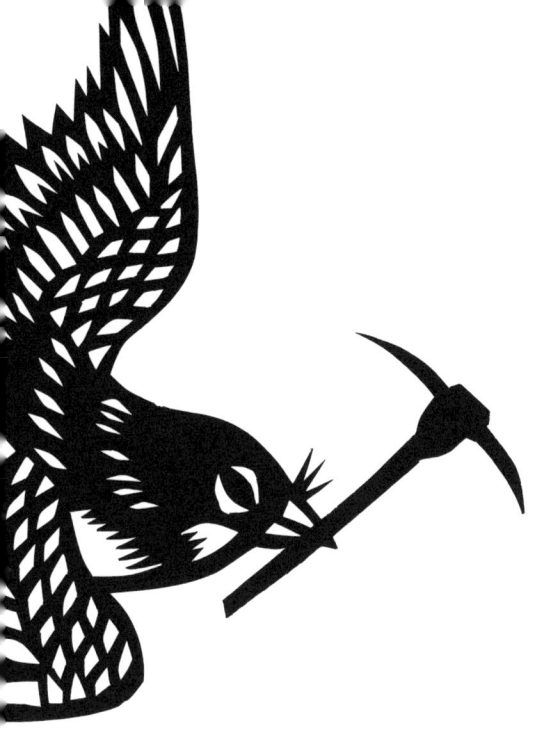
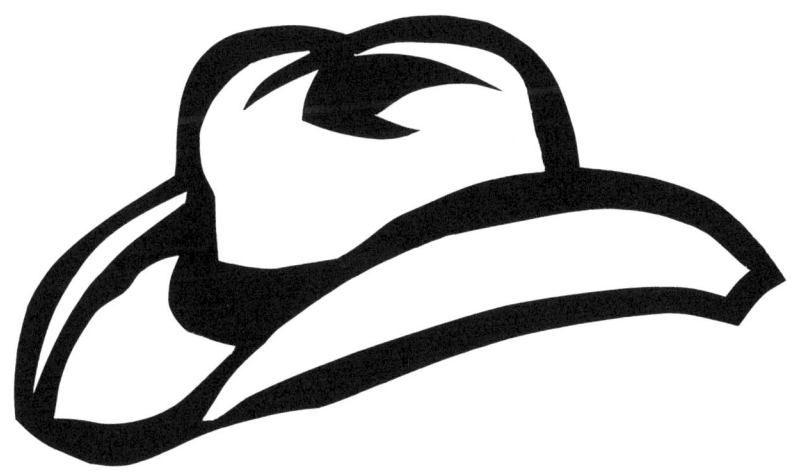

LUCKY LADY SALOON

Bartender pulling corked whiskey bottle from under the bar

Clem barely has time to take off her hat
stranger at the end of the bar calling out

Pour the lady a drink, this one's on me

Clem nods to the cowboy
Bartender, you can leave me the bottle

sound of ragged honky tonk piano
rustling dancing skirts
she shoots the whiskey back
face sour
      —stares—

Looking for company?

she drops his offer like a stone

How 'bout a smile?

Clem wishes he'd go away
why don't they ever just go away?

her silence grows sneer across his face

I know your kind
Think you're too good for a man like me

Clem clenches neck of bottle
struts her whiskey to a table on the other side of room

                            (oh whiskey)

now liquid hitting glass

Swinging image of Someone
black horse bounding from cliff

Cool heavy gun tucked into her thigh

Clem reaches under the table
tip of finger dragging
along the rough underside
trusting she will catch a star

she finds the etched groove of a star
one of hundreds she scratched into the wood
long ago when she was a small child

she traces the star in its entirety
moves to another,
smaller one, then
another, fingers
searching through dark
and stars
searching for the moon

       —the moon—

She closes her eyes

holds moon on the tip of her finger

        how still the night is

Saloon sounds fading away
Clem in the dark with her lonesome self
listening for animals, birds, bandits

massive stone sentinels wait with her for the next star to fall

she listens to the fire chewing the wood
is warmed by dying flame

      —flash of a star falling—

Clem's eyes open to a brilliant gaze

Someone is looking through smoke
waltzing through the ruckus of rough men's laughter

light in the room is remarkable
something unusually bright in these eyes

Clem's surprised, transfixed

Someone approaches

Would you like to dance?
Clem shakes her head no

Mind if I join you then?

Sure, Clem says
tipping her velvety cowboy hat just so

they sit there together
watching bodies sway on the dusty wooden dance floor
Someone shining with bright eyes

Clem darkening the room with her shadow
until the whiskey is gone

HER SHADOW DANCING

That's something they handed down, knowing how to dance in the middle of a storm. It was a matter of survival. No matter how tough times were, there was always dancing and laughter, though there was silence and loud voices too, and sometimes tears.

Once she was in bed, when there was a little time in between long hours of work and fretting about money, her folks would pull out a bottle, turn on some music and dance. Charley Pride, Hank Williams, Merle Haggard, Johnny Cash, Patsy Cline, Dolly Parton and Tammy Wynette. Sometimes they danced to the local country music station. It was on all of the time in the kitchen, even when no one was at home.

The walls of the trailer were paper thin, pressed particle board and endurance. The sounds of their love filled the trailer. Her mom laughing, but sometimes the sound of crying, and sometimes no voices, just shuffle shuffle step, shuffle shuffle step, until she was fast asleep.

STONE HORSE

Violet pulls the potash out of her pocket and gives it a good lick.
Salt on her tongue.   Deep familiar.   Birthstone

When her father gave her the jagged pink rock, it was the size of a man's fist.
                                                  Bloodstone

Now it is the size of a songbird's egg fitting comfortably in her front pocket.
                                                  Touchstone

Every day, her dad and the men who lived near went deep underground to mine potash from the land.   Hearthstone

Disappeared into pink hills.   Tombstone

Hard men they were.   Fieldstone and Ironstone

She tucks the salty rock back into her pocket, wanders through her studio, hammer in hand.

    How hard she has become.

She will sculpt a return from the cold desert, from this strange wandering.

>Sculpt a stone horse.
>Ride away

awake in the middle of the night—again. there's a kind of
violent tremble, a jerking motion moving through my body.
tip of my sharpie on paper soothing.

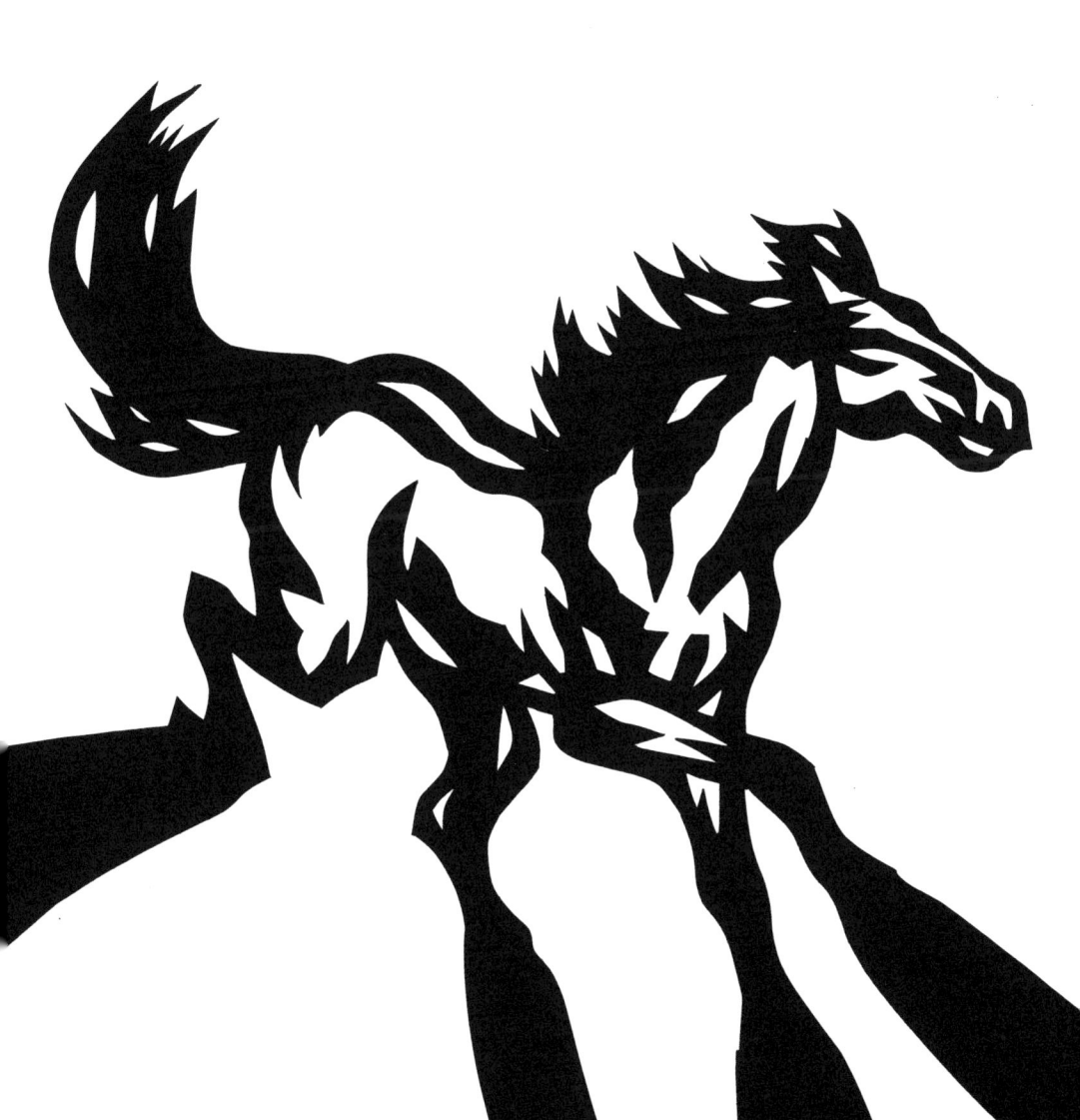

HERD OF WILD

Put the gun down Clem
Someone whispers in the dark

You don't need that fool thing with me
The bullet belt too

Clem laying the bullets on the table beside the bed

Let me show you my gun
It shines

You're scaring me Clem

Someone slips the gun away from Clem's palm

I'm not sleeping with you and a gun
I'll put it right here, next to the bullets

Clem lies awkward, naked
holds Someone
doesn't sleep, idea of love
herd of wild pounding on her chest

her eyes open. then close.
open again to the darkened room

furniture gradually takes shape
two end tables, a small dresser, single chair
edge of this bed

her gun, the bullets

sighing she rolls on her side
hands under sheet, hands over sheet
raise your hands high above your head

a warm leg across Clem's thigh
Someone draws Clem close, murmurs pleasure
body asleep, open

Clem draws back the sheet
naked skin, smooth muscle revealed

She wants to slide on top of Someone
—with her gun—

feel bare skin beneath her
enter armed into the landscape of sleep

Deep rumble of hooves
held in Clem's ribcage

something moving
      inside of her

she ignores it, blocks it

shuts
it
out

by sheer force of will
makes it seem as if it never was

some things are not meant to be remembered

Clem, a small hand tucked inside of hers

bare foot countermarch
red dirt road
trying not to collapse
into fault   opening earth

      listening for mother   (   )

Clem looking over her shoulder
feeling of someone
    coming to get her
    coming   all over her

old hotel, walking up wooden stairs
massive door strains to open

You?
woman nodding
girl slipping away
moving behind the woman with empty eyes
    —everything slowed down—

door closes, heavy metal bolt
hollow thud in Clem's chest

red fissure widens
dirt swallowing Clem
toes, feet, ankles, calves, thighs, sex, hips, chest, shoulders
can't move

loud crack of whip

        mother calling   (   )

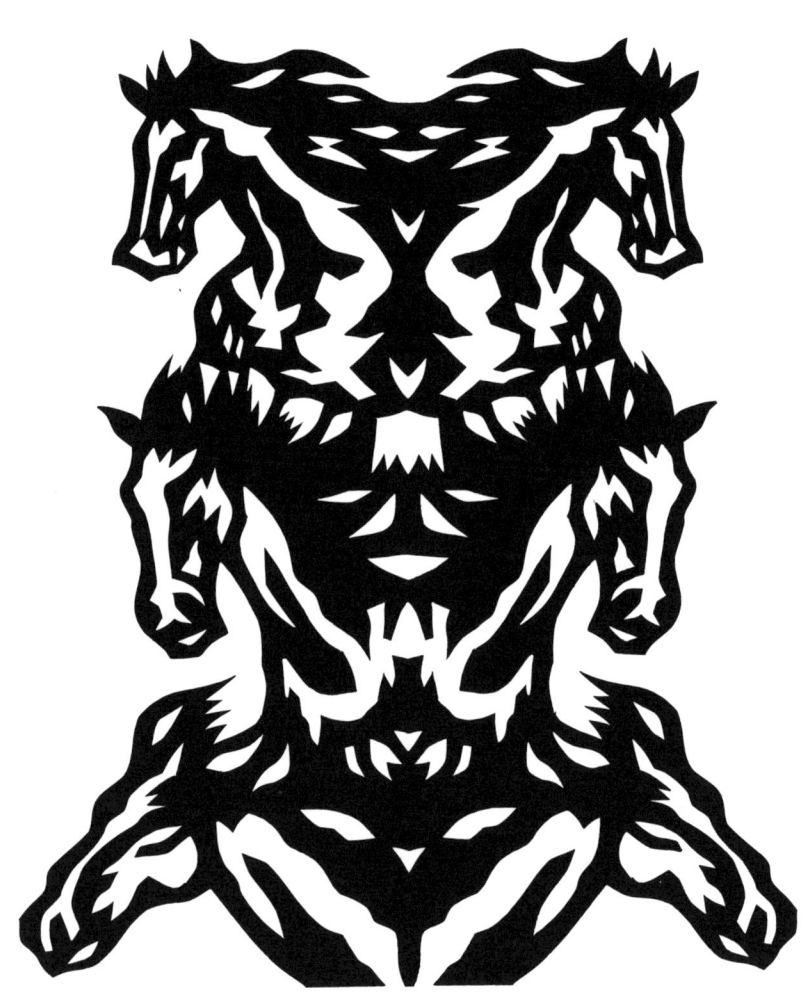

river carving an entire valley. can tears carve lonely stone?

INSIDE

Clem fingers the cool steel
—licks it—
opens mouth to barreled darkness

slips hand between legs
slides fingers deep into cunt
gun slipping too

ridges form
pink quivering of her insides
pushing up hard against the barrel

she tries to calls out
tries to call the girl

—Clem is gone—

With the light of morning
Someone wakes with slight image, whisper of sound
soiled red dress, distant howling

Clem, dead to the world
hand clutching gun
resting heavy on her stomach

low rumble, people in the room next door
walls creaking with the wind
a sparrow

        Someone pulls Clem close

Clem stirs, shifting her body   away

cold growing between them

Good morning
Morning

Clem rising from the bed

Why don't you stay awhile?

Look.

        hands raised

Don't fence me in.

Clem dresses.   Bullet belt on hips, hitches rig

        pausing at the door
        leaning against doorframe

        not knowing why

THE QUESTION OF BEING FENCED IN

Black marks on paper. Violet smudges each charcoal line with her finger, pushing it across the page, trying to find the end of the line. She tries to break the line with her blackened finger, pushes the charcoal upwards then down. The line will not break, it is now marked with vertical barbs. Strengthened by her attempts.

How quickly the line becomes a fence. Everyone seems fenced in by something, this is clear to Violet. Fenced into a territory, a place, owned by violence, history. Violet imagines these straight, rigid lines anchored into the land by force.

Her plot is surrounded by a series of fences. The fences are wooden, literary, charcoal, cinematic, barbed, cultural, emotional, steel, artistic, electric, historic, familial, stone.

Settlement fences laid down by those who have gone before her. Laid down into the land, into text, image, sound, in every line and word, laid down deep in her imagination.

Everything's been settled.

She turns to face the settlers, to all who have claimed land, water, resources. She meets farmers, cattlemen, miners, oilmen, face to face. She turns to face those who ride rough shod, the Indian agents, border guards, prison guards, minute men, police, military, vigilantes. She faces the power brokers, the bosses, the suits, the government, the bankers, the law.

She draws fences, trying to understand how they work. They've been laid on the landscape, but inside of her too. For so many years she has tried to dismantle them, but these fences go deep inside of her, down deep into the earth. These are smart fences detecting the slightest shift in soil, in memory, sensing every attempt to step outside of the plot laid down for her.

She gazes inward. Can't dig deep enough inside to where the horizon line must surely be, but she can still see the sky, above these towering fences.

Wide and blue.

She can still see. The sky.

in the desert you can remember your name — America

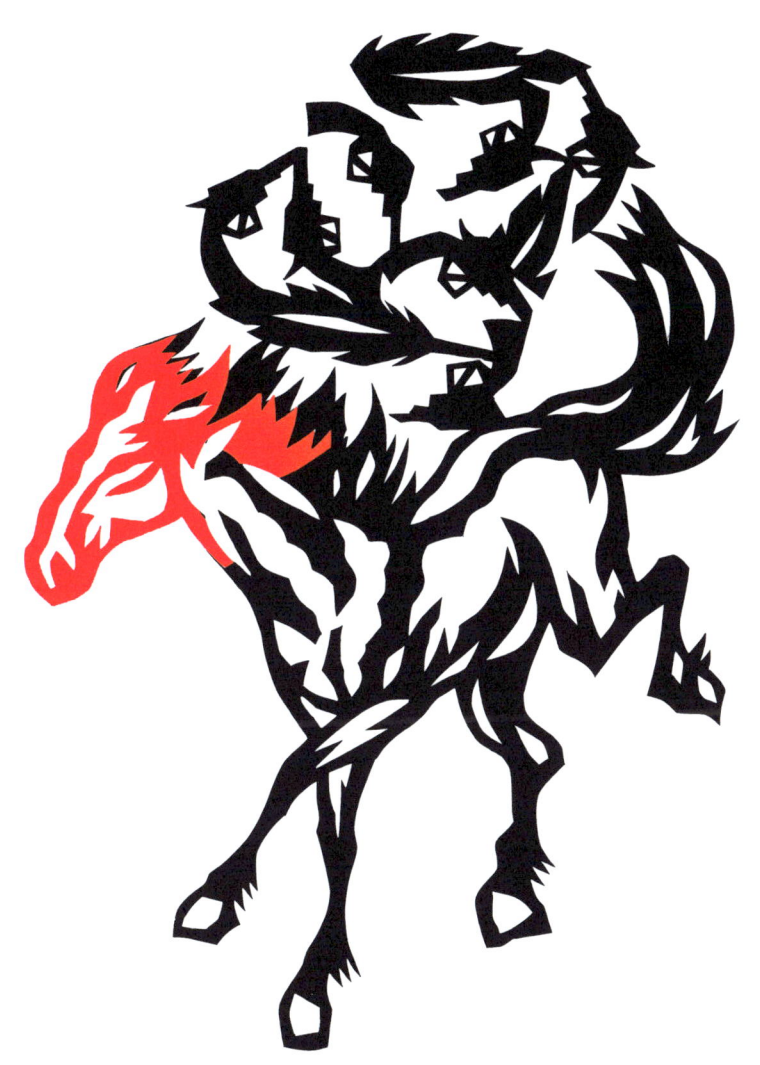

THUNDERING HOOVES

Someone gathers the rope lying at base of the tree
untangles it in the shade of green
releases hangman's knot

sets lynch rope spinning
lariat alive with the right touch

hangman's rope to trick rope
with the slip of a knot

vertical hoops grow larger, smaller
flat spin, rope kissing the ground
lifting dust into the air

whip
spin

rope filling with light
clockwise, then counter
whoosh
shoosh

Someone jumping in and out
of spinning loop of light

caught by her own shadow
Clem watches, rope intensifying

Join me,
Someone calls

Clem steps into illuminated rope
it moves up and down
encircling them

in this body spin, Someone pulls Clem close
                jumps   Clem's shadow

—rope a blur now—

dizzied, Clem can barely stand so close
bodies touching
lighted rope spinning

Can't tolerate tender
      needs gun: heavy dark feel of it

Clem wants to ride alongside Man with No Name
ride through gunfire
feel nothing but powerful
make the gun shine again

pulling the gun out
she spins it on her index finger
tosses it up into the air, nervous, elated
grabs the rope, spins around
catching the gun

I want to show you
Clem moves the gun to her open mouth

Watch it will sparkle as brightly as your eyes

                Clem holds it there

everything dropping away
even the ground they are standing on

Clem, her gun
Someone
lifting into sky.

mouth wide
cold steel

Close your eyes

Clem doesn't know if she's crying, laughing
knows only the sound of horses horses horses

pink dust covering them

smell of horse hair and sweat
hooves and mane

there, beside her
Someone's black horse

fistful of mane, leg over
hand reaching out
stealing away Clem's Colt
        her empty hand stinging

Hah! Hah!

Clem chases after tangled mess of lariat   trailing behind
eating dust

NIGHT SKY

Yippie yi Ohhhhh
Yippie yi yaaaaay

Someone, a stampede of wild

Lassoes tip of crescent moon
pulls it close, sets it free
galloping to the edge of stars
then, quick turn, thundering back
sky vibrating with light

Someone catches stars with teeth, head tilted back
launches them back into the sky
       —shooting stars—

swallows the smallest
can't stop laughing
touches rough ridges on neck

      lucky stars

plunges head into silky mane
squeezing thighs just enough

       to keep from falling

Girl watches Someone
herd of stone horses in night sky

knees pulled tight into her chest
coyote lying near, head tucked under tail

fire warming them

LIFTING STONE

Silence. Bare white walls. No windows, dim lights.

Violet sits in the centre of the room, at a small square oak table. An empty wooden chair across from her. Projected on the wall behind her is a silent video of Monument Valley. The projected landscape continually loops.

She waits for the next visitor to sit with her.
When someone arrives she picks up a book from under the table and reads:

Lifting Stone
Kiss my stone. She did.
Kiss my stone again she did.
Kiss my stone over and over and over again she did.
I have cherrystones.
Gentle clingstones.
Do you think about peachstones. We find them very beautiful.
It is not alone their colour it is their siltstones that charm us.
We find it a change.

Lifting stone is so strange.
I came to speak about it.
Selected hailstones. Thunderstones are good.
Change your name.
Question and tombstone.
It's raining. Don't speak about it.

My baby is a sunstone. I want to tell them something.
Inkstone and firestone. We have bought a great many rhinestones.
Some are moonstones. They have not been lighted.
I did not mention gemstones.
Exactly.
Actually.
Question and fieldstone.
I find the limestone very good.

Lifting stone, monumental.

Lifting stone stonily.

Doesn't that astonish you.

You did want me.
Say it again.
Bloodstone.

Lifting beside stone. Lifting kindly stone.

Sing to me I say.
Some women are stones not horses.

Lifting stone stonily.
Sing to me I say.

Lifting stone. Her horse.

After her performance, Violet gifts an artist book to the visitor.

    Repeat performance.

(performance was frighteningly intimate. wonder if gertrude ever visited monument valley, or stood on john ford's point, or ate stone soup. i doubt she ever ate stone soup.)

PRESSED FLOWERS

abolish avoid ban banish bar blackball blacklist block boycott bridle brush off cast off cast out censure chase awa clamp down close down cold shoulder condemn constrain crack down cramp crush curb curse cut dead cut off cut out damn denounce deny deport deprive deter disallow disband discard discharge discourage disinherit dislodge dismiss disown disperse displace dispose of dispossess divorce doom drive away drive out eject eliminate eradicate evacuate evict exclude excommunicate expatriate exile expel expulse extradite faze out forbid force out freeze out hinder hold back hold down ice out impede inhibit isolate kick out lock out obstruct ostracize oust pass up prevent prohibit proscribe push aside put down quash quell refuse reject relinquish remove repudiate restrict repress restrain rid rule out run out seclude segregate send away send packing sentence sequester show out shun shut down shut out silence snub snuff out spurn squash squelch steer clear of stigmatize suppress suspend turn out ward off withhold

One cold spring Violet and her mother started flowers from seed. Sunflower, bachelor button, black-eyed susan, sweet pea, purple cone flower, dotted blazing star, nasturtium, blue-eyed grass, silvery aster, crowfoot violet, queen anne's lace, and ironweed. This was in reckless disregard for her mother's usual no frills policy. Through the cold spring months they tended the seedlings. First they waited for shoots to push through the soil, tender true leaves folding open. They faithfully watered the young plants turning them every day so their stems would grow sturdy and straight. Once the seedlings were large enough they transplanted them into bigger containers of dirt. When the earth was warm they transplanted the plants into the flowerbeds Violet and her father had built. Every day they tended their garden, watering and deadheading the blooms, picking small bouquets for the kitchen table. On a long summer day with the garden in full bloom, they cut massive bouquets. They sat on a huge stone in the shade underneath a small stand of poplar trees. Violet's mother declared, "we are the rich ladies." They laughed together, flowers falling from their arms, heads tossed back, faces to the sky.

stones of all sizes slide across the desert floor leaving
mysterious traces: a line pressed in the hardened sand.
how did the sailing stone create the furrow?

(my line, a heavy stone furrow)

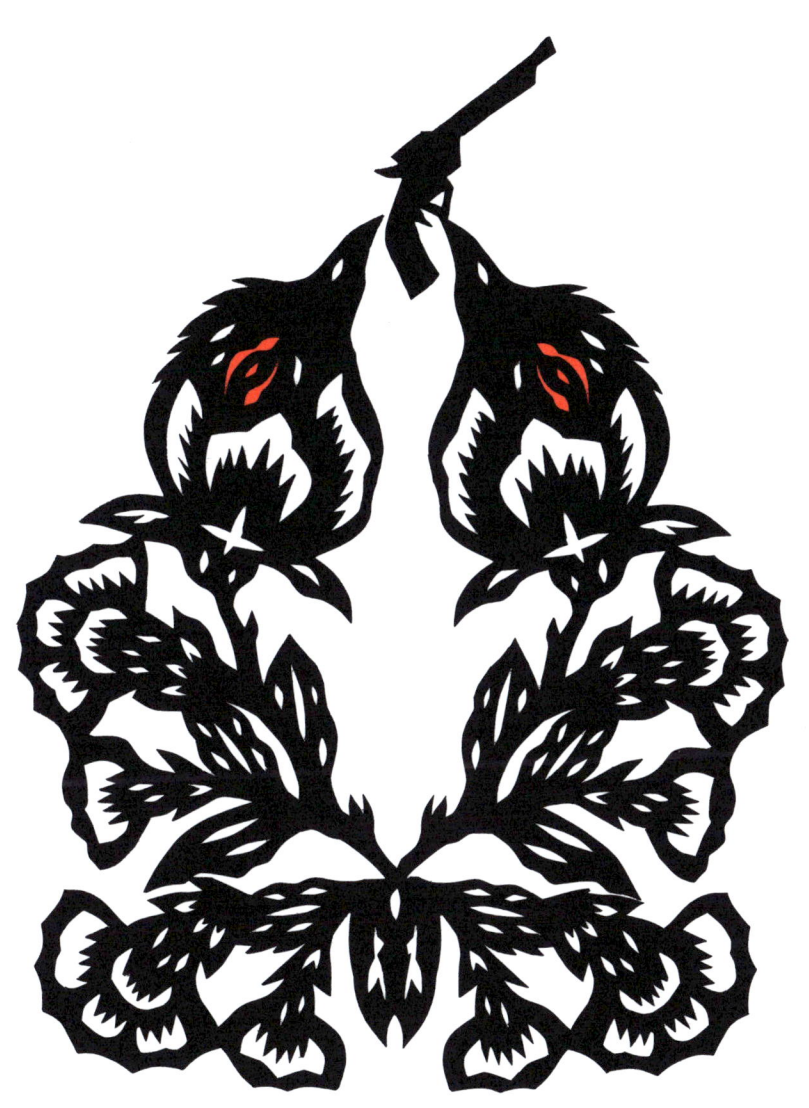

SHIFTING GROUND

Should she lay her ear to the ground?
look for broken twigs, horse shit?
follow her heart? patterns in clouds?

desert flowers are opened with the night's rain—
prickly pear cactus, sand lilies, spiderwort blooms

Clem rides close to the yellow cactus flowers
eyes searching, as if this is where she might find her gun
hidden among blooms and thorns

bird pokes its head
flies away
swooping, erratic

Clem and her horse trot behind
feathery body rests upon massive stone butte

tipping her hat back
Clem looks at bird, stone

In this moment
with bird perched on rock
Clem is filled with

      —mother—

tries to make sense of this
           bird flying away
              winged body vanishing

Clem leads her horse
up the craggy formation

           cutting

back
     forth

lessening steep incline

at the height of the butte she drops the reins
stands at pink edge

the entire valley stretching before her
again

    —feeling of mother—

    thousands of sand lilies
    slender white petals unfurling in rapid succession
    as if this might be their last moment to live,
    to open to the round orange mass
    melting into the land

    the scent is intoxicating

stone and petal and mother

land giving way with weight of family, history

the stone formations holding Clem
collapse dramatically
form aching canyon

stone crumbling

She and horse
sliding to the floor of this newly formed canyon

lipped by memory

SITE SPECIFIC

Just the dull thud of the hardened earth beneath her boots, Violet walks down the main street of the abandoned Western town. While the town is deserted, the buildings are remarkably well preserved. The feeling of this place also remains intact.

Everything was carefully constructed. In her mind she makes a list of the materials that were used. Wood, nails, glass, clay and shale. Each new building unquestioned, expansion assumed. No thought given to the first peoples of this place, to the land, or to the next generation and those who would also follow them.

There is no sign of green here, no sign of life. Uranium mining? Is that why the people have left? Was there another rush to the next thing, the next town? Did a few men gain wealth and move on while the others were left to scratch the dirt of nothing?

Violet walks around the old buildings. Stark structures built from felled trees and frontier dreams. She climbs up onto an old wooden box and looks into the Wild Horse Theatre. She can see the insides of the entire town here.

Most astonishing to her is that there are guns everywhere. Everywhere. Behind each door, over the bar, standing in corners, under the beds, in drawers, or sitting out in the open. Ammunition in closets and cupboards, in stores for sale.

She gathers the guns. Handles the guns. Lifts the guns, feels the weight of them in her hand. Handguns. Schofield single action, fast draw six shooter—some peacemakers—what kind of peace? Single action revolvers, henry repeating rifle, lever action rifle, pepper box pistols, Derringers, Remington, Mossberg and Winchester shotguns. Some still in their rigs.

She holds each gun properly as if she was going to fire it. Speaks the names of its parts —chamber, bolt, stock, firing pin, barrel— as if performance and language had the power to empty the gun of all deadly actions.

She sorts the handguns, into revolvers and pistols. Then the long guns into grenade launchers (single shot, multi-shot and automatic), rifles, shotguns and submachine guns. Separates the rifles. Bolt action, pump action, lever action, semi-automatic action, break (hinge) action. Then the shotguns with their smooth bore and front sights. Notices the weight of the submachine guns. Once the firearms are sorted, she constructs perfectly heaped piles of each type of gun on the wooden walkways on both sides of the dirt street.

Stepping into the middle of the road she digs the heel of her boot into the dirt, running it all the way down main street. Her calf and thigh ache with the exertion of digging the line in this way. She opens containers of black powder and trails the mixture of charcoal, sulfur and potassium nitrate into the rut of the line she has created, branching the powder out to the front of each building along the street.

Here on this line of gunpowder, she places a series of guns, increasing in gun power. She places an AK-47 and an AR-15 near the end.

Violet walks into the desert, into the pulsing sun, tired and thirsty. Returns in an M4 Sherman tank, parking it in front of the bank.

>She lights the line.

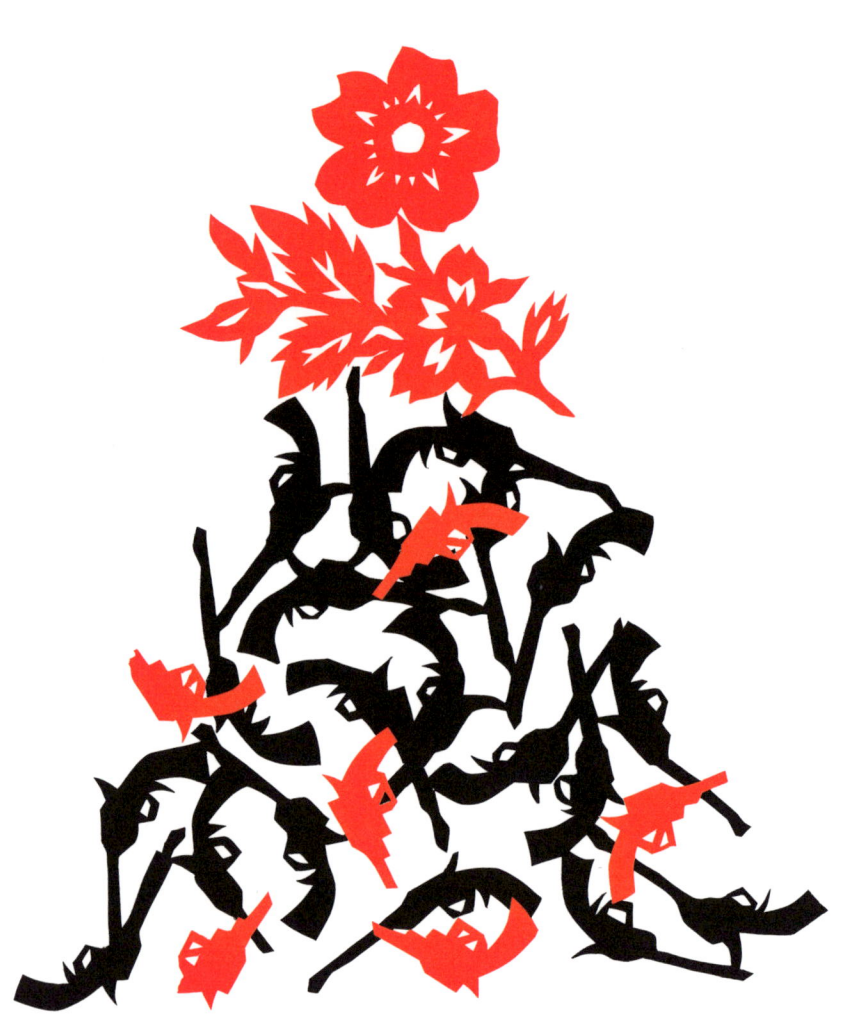

And I still miss Someone — Johnny Cash

DON'T TAKE YOUR GUNS TO TOWN

Road lined with embers
ardent vestiges of public buildings, the general store
bank, theatre
livery stable and blacksmith
saloon, laundry, barber
bath and dentist

town burning to the ground

she cannot see through to the blazing past
flames devouring story

massive wood timbers crash
horse hesitates, spooked

with every step
the pop
of a bullet
sharp
sudden

Bullet sounds explode
in her ears, mouth, chest

wounded?

dreaming?

horse
water pump
metal bucket
abandoned wagon

Clem slides off horse
hoping legs will hold

places bucket under spout
wraps hand around wooden handle
pumps slowly

       —no water—

she could just spit if she wasn't so dry
howl if she cared

She thinks about crying in a far off distant way
like it was something that might have happened
a long time ago

imagine me, all alone
falling to my knees, crying
someone rushing to my side

not damn likely

pumping, she silently pleads
swallowing dust and smoke

how far she has traveled to arrive here (again)

a single drop of blue wet
falls into empty bucket

       then
slow weep of water

bucket fills with cold, clear
she and horse drink thirstily

—ride away, ride away—

Clem unsnaps her shirt
strips it off
wrapping cotton around her hand like a glove
returns to the piles of weapons
guns burning through earth

one by one she collects hot angry guns
piles them into the wagon

murder of crows perch on the limbs of a single tree

Clem detects the slightest movement
draws her gun
maybe some poor critter survived the fire

there, behind the Sherman tank sitting in the middle of the street

Clem approaches the armored vehicle
Who's there? gun pointed

Girl appears from behind
dirty red dress, cowboy boots
coyote at her side

I've been waiting for you
You have?
Yup

Girl slightly taken aback by the cowboy full of holes
tries not to stare though them
light and fire coming through from the other side

What 'cha staring at?
Nothing
You alone kid?
Do I look like I'm alone? motions to coyote

You're not going to shoot us are you?

Clem lowers her gun
That mangy yodel pup?

I might kill a man
But I'd never kill a dog
wild or otherwise

They stood there awhile,
bullets popping around them

We should leave
Want to ride with me in the wagon?
Yah

The sound a mouth makes easing horses into motion
        sound of a wagon straining to carry a heavy load
        sound of flames behind them

You from this town?

Can't be from a town that burned to the ground, can ya?

"when you're able to distinguish the art of the horizon at the bottom of the frame, or the top of the frame, but not going right through the center of the frame. when you're able to appreciate why it's at the bottom you might make a pretty good picture maker."
— john ford to a young steven spielberg on the importance of art and the horizon line in making pictures.

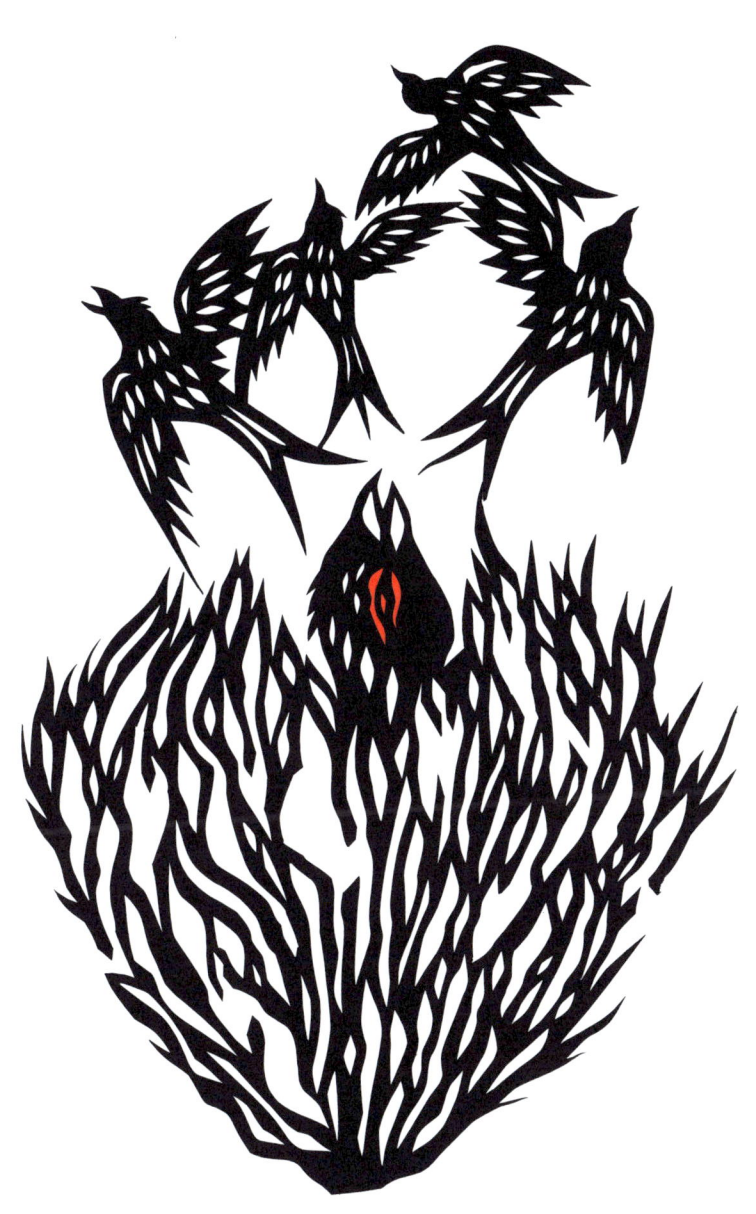

HORIZON

You're full of holes
Everything is
Lots of blood too
Yah

You might be dying, Girl says
Maybe I'm already dead

Could be, I don't know
I'm just a girl

Where are we going
Over there

Clem gesturing toward fractured horizon

Clem and Girl ride
        sun beating down

father's house
a mirage, wavering

Clem glances over her shoulder

Someone, Violet
approaching

Someone jumping into the wagon
slipping the reins from Clem's bloodied hands

Clem's body
lift lifting

over

Someone's shoulder

Someone laying Clem
down onto the ground

Dead girl kneeling close
her small hand holding Clem's

                        (i see stone horses running)

Didn't escape it, did I

Someone nodding
No, you didn't

Take my gun
Bullets too

You'll stop by when you're 'round these parts again?

Yes I will

You have the brightest eyes

I didn't get to say goodbye to my mom
I know Clem

My dad too
Yah

I've always been alone

Someone closing Clem's eyes.
Gently.

Violet digs deep into the ground
next to the grave of the dead bird
shovel scraping

earth sliced, opened to hold Clem's dead body

Someone, Violet
the dead girl

        —   silence   —

dirt and stone falling
from their hands

        covering her

Place daisies, johnny jump-ups, and violets on her grave

                        (last thing I wanted was for Clem to die)

Someone lays Clem's gun
leather belt of bullets

beneath the tree curved by the wind

THE SUN SETTING

Violet walks into the valley of pink rocks.

West. She is walking into the West.

There is a sun. It still sets.

She is thinking about the constant shift of colour. The deep sensation of warmth in this light. She stops, turns her face to the sun setting.

She leans into stone. Releases her full weight. She can feel the ridges running along the width of her back, sun and stone warming her. She rests here, gathering pieces of herself with each breath. Gust of wind quietly howls across the expanse, picking up dust. Quiet calm returns.

A condor glides by. Sharp piercing hiss. Its shadow passing over her.

She slides her palms across the rock, feeling the stone she is up against. Her fingers find tiny smooth holes of different sizes and shapes.

She turns to face the rock.

It is a towering sculpture with the shining presence of a full moon, rising as the sun sets. Massive stone sheets piled up on top of one another. Some of the stones stand slant, almost upright. Others lie flat. Streaks of uranium fall yellow from the sides. Stones stacked from the ground into sky. Haphazard. Precise.

Violet examines the vibrant surface. Colour shimmers from shades of pink to red to orange. Embedded in the stone are flecks of sparkle.

Some of the edges of the slabs are sharp, jagged. Some smooth.

The structure is riddled with holes, as if bullets ripped right through the rock and then over time, wind, rain, sun, animals wore the sharp edges into smooth unusual shapes. The holes grew larger, some big enough to put her fist through, her heart, her shoulder, her entire body. A large irregular hole opens into a particularly queer hollow.

She steps inside.

       (it is quivering, this stone, this land, with her touch)

WITH GRATITUDE

It has been my good fortune over the years to attend artist/writer retreats that have provided me with valuable time and support to create, think, and write. A great big thank-you goes out to the amazing artists and writers I have met at these retreats. My creative work and my life have been enriched by my participation in these temporary artistic communities. Thanks also go to retreat faculty that I have worked with: Greg Hollingshead (The Banff Centre Writing Studio), Daphne Marlatt and Nicole Brossard (Sage Hill Writing Experience), Steven Ross Smith, Fred Wah, and J.R. Carpenter (In(ter)ventions: Literary Practice at the Edge at the Banff Centre), Rosalie Favell and Huma Mulji (Mentoring Artists for Women's Art), Collective Members of Post Commodity, Candice Hopkins, and Anthony Kiendl (Plug In Institute of Contemporary Art Summer Residency).

Excerpts of *Quivering Land* first appeared in the article "Feminist Encounters with the Hollywood Western" in *Film, History, and Cultural Citizenship: Sites of Production,* edited by David Churchill and Tina Chen; and in the artist chapbook *Second dig,* published in Winnipeg by Kegan McFadden and Larry Glawson of As We Try & Sleep Press. The piece, "Lifting Stone," a queer remix of text stolen from Gertrude Stein's *Tender Buttons*, was performed at Plug In Institute of Contemporary Art Summer Residency (2010). I am thankful for these opportunities and interest in my work.

I am grateful to be working at a university where art and creative endeavours are valued alongside other scholarly practices. I would like to acknowledge funding from the University of Winnipeg Research Office Discretionary Grant Program. Yay! to those who worked for the inclusion of creative works in the University of Winnipeg Faculty Association Collective Agreement. A warm thank-you goes out to my fabulous colleagues and friends in the Women's and Gender Studies Department—Fiona Green, Angela Failler, Pauline Greenhill, Michelle Owen, and Liyana Fauzi—I greatly appreciate your support, sense of fun, and commitment to creating a scholarly work environment that is welcoming to artists. For engaging conversations and generous feedback on early versions of the text, I thank Heather Milne, Colin Smith, Jeanne Randolph, Eileen Myles, and Catherine Hunter. Thank you for sharing your valuable time and insights.

In my work at the University of Winnipeg Institute for Women's and Gender Studies I have had the privilege of working alongside many people who inspire me to continue on the frontlines of a collective struggle to make a better world. A warm heart-filled thanks goes out to the Coalition of Families of Murdered and Missing Women in Manitoba, who have shown me how to keep searching for those who are missing in the face of denial, indifference and discouragement. A shout-out also goes to FemRev, the young feminist collective based in Winnipeg whose dynamic feminist spirit and activism helped to sustain me during long periods in my studio sitting in front of the computer. Fist high in the air! Viva! Viva! Viva!

For interest, valued conversations and encouragement during the long road of writing this book, a heartfelt thank-you to: Elizabeth Ruth, Shannon Olliffe,

Ariel Gordon, Peter Kulchyski, Praba Pilar, Janet Sarson, Nadin Gilroy, Michelle Meagher, Chandra Mayor, Alison Calder, Warren Cariou, Milena Placentile, Debra Parkes, Rachel Zolf, Marjorie Poor, Lorri Neilsen Glenn, Judy Davidson, Damien Luxe, Amber Dawn, and my FB friends! A shout-out also to Liz Duffy Adams for sharing her magical New York desk during my editing process. Liba Scheier, I remember you too.

It was a pleasure to collaborate with artist Paul Robles. I brought *Quivering Land* to Paul and he responded with evocative and beautiful hand-cut images. Our connection grew through shared family stories and led to a continued collaboration. In the spring of 2013 Jennifer Gibson (Gallery 1C03, University of Winnipeg) approached me to exhibit artistic work from *Quivering Land* in an exhibit, MY MONUMENT / POP UP BOOK, from March 6 to April 5, 2014, with Paul Robles, Steven Leyden Cochrane, and Cam Bush.

Through the documentary film, *The Return of Navajo Boy* by Groundswell Educational Films, I learned about the hundreds of abandoned uranium mines in Monument Valley and how this reckless corporate and government disregard has poisoned the land, air, water and people of this place. I learned about the remarkable environmental justice work of Elsie Mae Begay, various Navajo communities, and Navajo grandmothers. I learned that this injustice and toxic mess from the past continues to fatally harm those living on their traditional territories today. The informative book by Judy Pasternak, *Yellow Dirt: An American Story of a Poisoned Land and a People Betrayed*, further informed me about this toxic legacy.

I want to thank my comrades at Arbeiter Ring Publishing editorial collective—Peter Ives, Esyllt Jones, Kathleen Olmstead, John K. Samson, and Todd Scarth—for their determination to maintain a press that remains solidly committed to politics. These are the kind of people you want in your community: political, caring and hard-working. A big thank-you goes to Sarah Michaelson for the fine copy edit. And for transforming the word files into a thing of beauty, I am grateful to Mike Carroll for designing a spectacularly gorgeous book. Every press should have someone like Rick Wood in the office; competent and a delight to work with, Rick kept things beautifully organized and moving along smoothly. I want to also thank John K. Samson for his insightful editorial suggestions and for insisting that books must be beautiful objects.

The artistic vision of *Quivering Land* was nourished through the editorial guidance, skill, and wisdom of poet Betsy Warland. Our relationship during the editing process was absolutely crucial. She brought a deep knowledge of artistic process, intuition, generosity, support, encouragement, and clarity to our work together. Her ability to connect deeply with my text and her utmost respect for knowledge that comes from experiences of silence and exile helped me to more deeply trust my process and the poetic narrative as it unfolded. I am deeply grateful. Thanks Betsy!

Finally, my deepest gratitude to Jarvis Brownlie, whose unswerving insistence that I pursue my artistic practice and take liberties with my text helped me to be uncompromising in my vision. With you I gain courage to stand tall in the face of injustice and violence. Thanks love for riding beside me up every hill, through every shadow and lonely valley, always reminding me to turn my face to the sun. It is such a deep pleasure to share with you our passions for art, music, feminist politics, and history. Our big sky love inspires me every day, as does our shared desire that we might all walk more gently on Turtle Island.

BIOGRAPHIES

Roewan Crowe

Artist and theorist Roewan Crowe is energized by acts of disruption, transformation and the tactical deployment of self-reflexivity. She has a particular interest in wounded landscapes and questioning what it means to be a queer, feminist settler living in Winnipeg/Turtle Island. Recent work includes: *digShift* (ongoing), a decolonizing and environmental reclamation project using site specific performance and multichannel installation to explore the shifting layers of at an abandoned gas station; and Queer Grit, a stop-motion animation that asks, "how can you be Queer on the prairies when your dad is John Wayne?" Her scholarly work seeks to open meaningful encounters with art and explore new feminist art practices. Her longstanding community practice is concerned with building engaged feminist/queer/artist communities, and in addressing the reality of Murdered and Missing Indigenous Women in Canada. She is an Associate Professor in the Women's and Gender Studies Department at the University of Winnipeg and Director of The Institute for Women's & Gender Studies.

www.roewancrowe.com

Paul Robles

Paul Robles is a Canadian artist based in Winnipeg. Born in the Philippines, he immigrated to Canada with his family at the age of four. He holds a Bachelor of Fine Arts degree from University of Manitoba and Bachelor of Arts degree (Sociology) from the University of Winnipeg. Paul has exhibited nationally and internationally, including Outpost Contemporary Art, Los Angeles; Malaspina, Vancouver: The New Gallery, Calgary: Rideau Hall (Governor General Selected), Ottawa; Doris McCarthy Gallery, Toronto; as well as Plug In ICA and The Winnipeg Art Gallery. His work has been featured as a CBC ArtSpots and has appeared in *Border Crossings*, *The Globe and Mail*, and *Walrus*. In 2011, Robles was showcased as part of ART Paris in the Grand Palais; in "My Winnipeg" group exhibition in Paris and Sete, France; at the Drake Hotel in Toronto; and at Julia Saul Gallery in New York City.

paulrobles.blogspot.ca